A TRIBUTE TO TULIPIA

CHIARA TALLUTO

DEDICATION

For my daughters, Ava and Stella. Don't ever be afraid to be a Tulip. Stand up for what is right!

#BeATulip

For each **A Tribute to Tulipia** paperback purchased, I will donate a portion of the proceeds to **Stand for the Silent,** an anti-bullying organization that travels to schools to address the issue of bullying with an engaging, factual and emotional methodology. Their mission is to inform students and staff about bullying awareness along with the real devastation it causes. Let's keep "I AM SOMEBODY" Stand for the Silent © program alive. For more information, please check out: https://standforthesilent.org/.

WELCOME TO THE JADE OASIS

Her name was Tulipia. She lived in the Jade Oasis, a forest of tangled vines, weeds and shrubs.

Tulipia was an only tulip. Orphaned at a young age, she lost her parents after they'd been extracted from the Oasis. Tall and lean, she soared over many of her nemeses.

Nemeses, you ask?

Most of the foliage around Tulipia was jealous of her beauty, height and intelligence. Smarter than her rivals, Tulipia predicted the weather, hummed many tunes and had the prettiest, smoothest pink petals.

Though one wouldn't know by looking at her, Tulipia suffered from loneliness. None of the other greenery spoke to her or wanted to be her friend. Envy, animosity, or just plain hate, Tulipia couldn't tell you; as she was often talked about behind her back, pranked on, and never given her proper share of nutrients from the soil.

To overcome her anxiety, she created fairy tales in her mind, dreaming of fields of pink and purple tulips—cousins and distant family dancing in the afternoon light. Regardless of these trials, the sun always shone upon her, the moon smiled at her, and the stars twinkled for her.

Being an only tulip is not always bad. Her mother, Temple, said she was a miracle seed born out of the love shared with her husband, Titan.

Tulipia was showered with affection, educated on various topics taught only to exotic flowers and trained to do the right thing for others: like offering coverage to rodents when it rained and giving nectar to bees and butterflies that stopped by to rest on her beautiful petals.

When she was sprouting, her father said God blessed her with a special ability to flourish anywhere. Despite how lucky she'd been, Tulipia still felt unaccepted in her surroundings.

The day her parents were ripped from the ground, Tulipia was miraculously spared by a mere few inches. Not knowing why, she believed in her heart that she must persevere and carry on. It is what her mother and father would have wanted her to do.

With that revelation, Tulipia dug her roots deeper, grew and grew, relying not on food alone, but by living out her parents' wisdom.

She felt in her heart that goodness would come one day, and so she continued to blossom even amongst her enemies.

****

While being friendless was an issue in the wilderness, so was safety. Sundown was a perilous time in the Jade Oasis. The animals were out and in search of food. Tulipia's estranged neighbors sought shelter under her because of her long stalk. If the carnivores couldn't find anything to eat, they'd turn to the foliage and shrubbery to fill their bellies.

One evening, a wolf was trampling through the forest. Tulipia could hear him panting and smelled his sweaty flesh as he neared. She stood very still even as the west wind tickled her petals. The other greenery took her cue to do the same. However, with each heavy footstep coming closer and closer, that security was minimized.

Screams emitted through the air as the wolf found some herbs, ripping them from the earth, munching contentedly. Tulipia squeezed her eyes shut, wanting to dismiss the cries for help.

"Please don't let me be eaten," she prayed.

Through the brush, a few feet away, an adorable bunny skipped about, rubbing its nose in the rose bushes. Tulipia tried swaying her almond-shaped mini leaves to get the hare's attention, but it didn't see her. The shrubs noticed the rabbit but were too afraid to say anything or move.

Tulipia turned toward a couple of tangled vines. "What are you doing lying around? Prick that animal!" she hissed.

The vines ignored her.

Creeping slowly and squashing a few weeds in the dirt, the wolf spat out parsley as he spotted the little rabbit.

"Oh no!" Tulipia cursed. Spinning around, she yelled to the other foliage, "Won't anyone help the poor bunny?"

Still, no one heeded her pleas. The sunflowers shielded their seeds, the rose bushes folded over, and the lilac trees pretended to be dead.

The ugly beast suddenly pounced upon Tulipia, as he eyed the bunny with a growling hunger. And then something strange happened. It had been an overcast day and as evening approached, it looked like it would rain. The clouds mysteriously moved and a full moon appeared, shining its rays on Tulipia and the wolf.

The wolf sniffed the air. The fragrance of her petals had entranced him. *This flower looks so scrumptious. I'll just have myself a bite.* He licked his chops.

The hare raised its nose from the bushes and saw the wolf. Realizing the danger, it took off hopping through the forest.

The hairy creature towered over Tulipia, saliva dripped from its mouth. She tightened every single muscle in her body, knowing the end of her life was near. "If he devours me, then so be it. I will save the rest of the shrubbery from being eaten," she contemplated.

The wolf howled, ready to sink its teeth into Tulipia. All at once, rose thorns flew into the air, stabbing the wolf's left foot. Falling to the ground, he winced in pain.

Sunflower seeds blasted into the wolf's face, poking his eyes. The vines jumped in, wrapping his hind legs. The wolf tried to fight off the greenery rebellion, but couldn't find the strength to do so. Finally, he untangled himself and limped away.

A loud cheer rang throughout the Oasis. The big bad wolf was gone and most of the vegetation was saved. Tulipia breathed a sigh of relief. She had been rescued and was thankful to her fellow foes.

After the Jade Oasis quieted down, the hare emerged from behind an oak tree. Surprised, all the foliage turned their attention to him.

He cleared his throat, "You have all erred by treating Tulipia harshly. She was willing to sacrifice her life so that you can have yours. She is to be respected and preserved."

The greenery humbly bowed down to her in apology.

"What's this?" she whispered.

The rabbit stood on its back legs. "Tulipia, you have always honored your mother and father through your actions. Thank you for demonstrating what bravery looks like. I'm also grateful for those few that came forward to help before it was too late."

Tulipia was shocked at what she heard and saw. Her courageous effort to save her neighbors was a simple and selfless attempt at keeping something bigger protected.

The hare concluded, "You are one big forest family. Act like it. Help each other out."

More cheers echoed through the Oasis. The rabbit nodded toward Tulipia and sauntered off. From that day on, all the wild shrubbery blossomed and worked together to protect their blessed forest.

***

Many years passed. The Jade Oasis flourished with vibrant greenery. Tulipia was in good health, but she was aging, her younger days just a blur in the wind.

Alone and without a life partner, Tulipia didn't want to gripe. Her mother, Temple, had said that not complaining should be a virtue. She snickered, remembering her mom's wisdom. *Is being lonely a virtue too?*

***

All was calm until one year when a terrible winter season fell upon the Oasis, freezing ninety percent of the foliage. The glacial cold lasted forty days and forty nights. Tulipia braced herself with every ounce of strength she could muster, even while giant icicles formed on her petals and stalk. It was a miracle she had sustained the frigid temperature while her counterparts snapped and cracked, falling to the earth.

When the snow melted, much of the dead shrubs and vines littered the soil like strewn garbage. The smell of deceased greenery made Tulipia sick for days until it became one with the soil; leaving only a barren land. Experiencing this traumatic circumstance, Tulipia succumbed to a deep depression and never uttered a word for a few years.

The adorable bunny that had once hopped in the forest was no longer little. He had grown old and had barely survived the natural disaster as one of his legs had frozen and fallen off. Hobbling on one leg, the bunny tried to restore hope and normalcy among the remaining shrubbery, but it was useless. The whole forest was in shock. Nothing would ever be normal again. And so, a hush blanketed the Oasis.

One morning, the rustle of fresh flora and vegetation arriving in the Oasis shook the swathed silence. They were being planted in the same soil as the original foliage that had perished.

The migrated shrubs were foreign-looking, they spoke unfamiliar languages. Tulipia and her pals didn't understand their new neighbors. It took weeks and months for the residents to acclimatize to life in the Oasis.

The hare, seeing an opportunity to gain confidence from the foliage, often returned to facilitate meetings between the native greenery and the immigrant thickets about the rules and laws of the Oasis. The immigrant shrubs didn't want to follow laws that had been in place before the wintry apocalypse. Instead, they wanted to establish their own customized rules and tenets.

It was a disastrous time, communication was squandered among the plant life, and it frustrated Tulipia to be living in this environment. She wished to have passed away along with many of her closest mates.

When Tulipia was younger and disliked the circumstances of the forest, the shrubs and vines still tried to work out their differences to find commonality for the good of the Jade Oasis. The shrubbery had changed; she had no control over the outcomes that might occur.

Tulipia was elderly and had missed her youthful years, unable to produce the next generation of Tulips. Feeling like a failure, she prayed feverishly to God for any kind of miracle for change in the Oasis. There were many plants and shrubs against her comrades, and the rabbit, once a respected voice in the forest, was ignored. Things weren't looking too good in this beautifully landscaped terrain.

Until...

An exotic flower was planted near her. It was a male that had traveled from a faraway land across two oceans. He was small in stature, round, with long lavender and yellow arms, and blue, white, and purple spears. His eyes were a deep shade of violet. The flower introduced himself as Rishonich (pronounced ree-SHAWN –ich).

They struck up a conversation. Though Rishonich appeared young and agile and spoke softly, Tulipia learned he would mature in a matter of weeks. He was an old soul and since his lifespan would be brief, he intended to make the best of it.

Soon enough, he grew old. He'd spent the last few weeks listening to stories from Tulipia and other nearby foliage about the Jade Oasis prior to the drastic changes since the current state of the forest had turned perverse and spiteful.

Rishonich shared stories about his upbringing, in a land that was colorful and bright where every flower was the same, while in the Jade Oasis; there was a blending of vines, shrubs and flowers.

Tulipia enjoyed learning from her neighbor. Though their backgrounds were dissimilar, she found it comforting to be around a flower that was closer to her age.

A friendship developed which led to a more serious relationship. Unbeknownst to the surrounding greenery, Tulipia and Rishonich fell in love.

Quietly and miraculously, surrounded by a chaotic revolution ensuing between the native and immigrant shrubbery, a special flower was born. It was a birth between two blossoms that were not only different species, but too advanced in age to even conceive.

When it became known that a bud was born, it sparked more controversy in the forest. There were those that were with Tulipia and Rishonich, and those that were against them. It had become personal.

A beautiful male seedling sprung, his name was Nevanobry (pronounced NEH-vin-OH bry). He was spherical like his father and had blue and purple glistening petals like his mother.

Nevanobry bloomed. Tulipia and Rishonich promised to raise their little sprout to be honorable in all his actions. They took it upon themselves to be role models and good citizens in the Oasis. She and her husband were on a mission to repair the community by educating the greenery about different ways to unite with each other for the purposes of safety and security within the forest.

With all the mayhem going on, more wild animals wandered into the Oasis, making it crowded. With every trampling of greenery, more was replanted. It was an ongoing cycle of plant life and plant death.

Tulipia and Rishonich spent many nights strategizing and praying for wisdom. There were constant protests and deaths shrouding the Oasis.

"Is this effort worth it?" Tulipia pleaded.

"Yes, we have to try harder to help our offspring to survive."

"But what if we fail?"

Spinning his spears, Rishonich said, "If we do nothing, we have failed. It is our duty to teach Nevanobry to be strong and stand up for what is right. Didn't you do that long ago?"

Tulipia nodded, "You are correct. I've tried. The forest of then is not the forest of now."

Rishonich wrapped his arms around his bride. "Agreed, my love. The times may be different, but the desires of our adversaries have not changed."

Nevanobry sprouted and watched his parents in action, absorbing and learning from them, while the killings continued among the shrubbery and the animals, causing havoc in the forest.

Tulipia schooled Nevanobry. She reminded her blossom, "If something happens to your father or me, you must continue with this mission."

Nevanobry smirked, "Oh Mother, you worry too much. Why do you have to be so dramatic?"

"Do what is right! That is all."

The wise old Tulip also made her bud memorize **five** key points to surviving in the Jade Oasis:

1. Respect history, even if you don't agree with it.

2. Get along with your rivals.

3. Don't complain; set your focus to complete.

4. There is no shame in asking for help.

5. Do the right thing.

Meanwhile, fear and anxiety continued to torment the young and the elderly in the Oasis.

***

Months later, one early morning, Nevanobry awoke to find his mother and father and many of the Oasis allies gone. They had been plucked out of the earth; vacant holes remained where once his mother and father's roots were knotted.

Nevanobry cried, "They've vanished! All of them! Why...Oh, why?"

Even the hare had disappeared.

This was a turning point for the Jade Oasis because what remained were two groups of foliage: Those wanting order and those against it.

Grief plagued young Nevanobry. He looked to the elders of the community for help, but they were frightened of the riots and fatal retaliation, and so they turned their stalks away from him.

Expectation and pressure lay upon him to carry on what his mother had pursued years earlier, and what his parents had tried to do. He requested approval from the greenery to assume command and he was nominated to be their leader.

Nevanobry was convinced he could reinstate order. *I must! That is what my mom told me to do.* So he set out to study his allies and enemies in search of a better system of living and working together. The budding flower poured over documentation from his parents and notes from the old rabbit.

The process took months, but he persisted and read, interviewed, and observed the flowers around him. What he found was that **power** was at the core of all the animosity taking place. It was a game of who would be the controller and who would be controlled.

Nevanobry, the appointed leader, created committees between the two sets of groups and encouraged them to craft their own laws. He then took those laws and combined them. This consolidation took decades to organize and the groups disagreed with him on every point.

Meanwhile, the fighting continued and Nevanobry's life was constantly in danger. But he persisted in standing up to his enemies because that is what Tulipia had always done. He would honor that until all the work was completed. *This is my promise. There has to be unity!*

Eventually, Nevanobry grew old too—while dedicating his life for the common good of all the greenery in the forest, a mission he took seriously. After years of sacrificing and being bullied, he realized creating a common good for *all* was a stretch, so he broke down the laws, forming territories within the Oasis. Each territory was responsible for upholding order within that area and as new foliage migrated into the Oasis, they were given rules to abide by.

Nevanobry appointed smaller committees that made sure each specific territory supported their laws. The tired blossom worked hard trying to keep his parents' passion alive until the life went out of him.

Nevanobry was removed, but nothing was ever replanted in its place. Instead, the soil was turned into a memorial.

Here stood an exotic flower named Nevanobry. Born by two dissimilar species, the bud flourished with one goal in life: to make the forest a better place to live. He did so, not to compete or argue, but on the principle of standing up for what is right. He honored his mother, Tulipia, a pioneer who would rather have stood out than fit it.

"Never stop the fire that burns within you."

THE END

It started with a picture, a picture of a tulip standing tall and confident surrounded by tangled brush and shrubbery. The greenery in the background accenting its beautiful pink petals caught my eye while on a hike with my daughters. The sun poking through the trees cast a glow of holiness about her that no camera could ever capture. She reminded me of a female, I named her Tulipia. And so a story began to stir in my mind, one that cannot be ignored. I knew I had to write this down.

It had been a tough season of bullying incidents for both my girls, so I tried instructing my children about standing up for what's right as well as doing the right thing for others. This sudden inspiration was God's gift of another means of explanation.

In this tale, there are four main characters: A tulip, a hare, a blossom, and a wolf. They live in a forest, the Jade Oasis. As I thought more about the characters and their habitat, the symbolic meaning of what they represent in their fictional world gave me the clarity to relate to ours.

So, what do a hare, a tulip, a blossom, and a wolf represent?

<u>The Jade Oasis</u>. The place where you live. Your town, community, neighborhood. All different cultures mixed in together living out their dreams or just coexisting.

<u>The Tulip</u>. Tulipia is like you and me. We aren't able to choose our parents, and learning comes from those with whom we associate. If given the correct life lessons, one can flourish even in the worst environments.

<u>The Hare</u>. Life can harden us after years of emotional and physical abuse. The hare is that mercy button we all have within each of us if we can learn to tap into it. Forgiveness is difficult, but showing mercy can move you to heal.

<u>The Wolf</u>. Every commercial, every magazine/newspaper article, and every post on social media often shows the "me" side. We live in a culture of wants. A wolf acts on its animal instinct because that is how it was made. Humans, by nature, are nurturing, but if the world keeps instilling a selfish instinct in each of us, it becomes part of our being.

<u>The Blossom</u>. Nevanobry—is the good son. He is the dreamer, the princess or prince in all of us, who, gifted with a talent, will work selfishly and tirelessly to achieve a goal. Whether he or she succeeds is not the point, but rather the effort to do it and put it into action is what counts. *Efforts do count*!

THE MEANING OF THE NAMES

As a writer, I never set out to write words with symbolic meaning. Sometimes it happens and sometimes it doesn't. The more I thought about this story, the more I've realized just how important it was to share it with my kids. I hope you'll do the same.

Tulipia: My own made up name to represent a tulip.

Temple: English Origin. Means "Sanctuary."

Titan: Greek Origin. Means "Land of the giants."

Rishonich: *Rishon* - A Hebrew name that means "the first." *Ichiro* - A Japanese name that means "first born son."

PRONUNCIATION: ree-SHAWN-ich.

Nevanobry: *Nevan* - This is the anglicized version of an Irish name meaning "little holy one." *Dobry* - This Polish name means "good, kind."

PRONUNCIATION: NEH-vin DOH-bry.

References:

http://babynames.net/
https://www.babynames.com/

INCREASING YOUR VOCABULARY

Reading is such a rich experience. Sometimes, you might come across words that you aren't familiar with, or know their definition.

Below, I compiled a short list of words you can look up in a dictionary.

Nemeses	Squandered
Revolution	Commonality
Foliage	Revelation
Orphaned	Ensuing
Erred	Havoc
Gripe	Torment
Muster	Flourish
Glacial	Migrated
Strewn	Immigrant
Barren	Foe
Succumbed	Adversary
Apocalypse	Blossom

NEXT STEPS

Dear Reader,

If you've enjoyed **_A Tribute to Tulipia_**, I would love it if you would help others enjoy this tale, too.

Here are some ways you can help spread the word:

Recommend it. Help other readers find this story by recommending it to friends, writing groups, reading groups, book clubs, and discussion forums.

Share it. Let other readers know you've read it by posting a note on social media pages.

Review it. Very important. Good, bad, or ugly, please tell others about this story. Review it on your favorite book sites: _Amazon_ and _Goodreads_.

#BeATulip

Your support of my writing endeavor is greatly appreciated.

Be sure to check out Chiara Talluto's other novels:

Love's Perfect Surrender. A Christian romance about a troubled married couple who lose the "us" part of their relationship after a failed miscarriage and still birth, until, the miraculous birth of their daughter, born with a congenital limb deficiency, who graces their lives shaking their core beliefs in hopes of making peace and letting love in.

Petrella, the Gillian Princess is a Middle-Grade fairy tale that interweaves themes similar to *The Little Mermaid, Cinderella, Tangled, Sleeping Beauty*, and *Noah's Ark*. It's about a courageous young princess who defies rank and authority to follow her heart. It is a story of hope, bravery, and triumph. This story can be used as a discussion piece about the importance of making solid, moral decisions, and understanding the consequences that result from those decisions, as well as an effective teaching tool to help explain all the elements that go into making a story, a story. And, it is meant to be enjoyed by all readers young at heart, but especially aimed at those children who read middle grade fiction: Ages 8 –13.

She Made It Matter. An Inspirational fiction about one woman's fight to regain sobriety, find salvation, and earn forgiveness after years of guilt from being abandoned by her mother and then losing her brother to cancer, a struggle to vanquish the demons of her past and make her life right again.

ABOUT THE AUTHOR

Chicago-born, a full-time mother and author, Chiara Talluto, is known as the *Master Storyteller* in her household. She has a passion for writing about people who struggle with decisions and conflicts that arise in their lives.

Currently, Chiara is hard at work penning other stories. When she's not writing, she is either reading or playing mommy with her two daughters. Her motto is: *Live, laugh and cry.*

To learn more about Chiara and her published works, please go to: www.chiaratalluto.com. She will gladly answer any questions you may have about Tulipia. Feel free to drop her a line.

For each **A Tribute to Tulipia** paperback purchased, I will donate a portion of the proceeds to **Stand for the Silent,** an anti-bullying organization that travels to schools to address the issue of bullying with an engaging, factual and emotional methodology. For more information, please check out: https://standforthesilent.org/.